Book 1

THE TOP-SECRET DIARY OF CELIE VALENTINE

Friendship Over

Julie Sternberg
illustrated by Johanna Wright

bmp

Boyds Mills Press   An Imprint of Highlights   Honesdale, Pennsylvania

Boyds Mills Press
An Imprint of Highlights
815 Church Street
Honesdale, Pennsylvania 18431
Printed in the United States of America
ISBN: 978-1-59078-993-3
Library of Congress Control Number: 2014939248
First edition
The text of this book is set in Zemke Hand ITC Std.
The illustrations are done in pen and ink.
Book Design by Robbin Gourley
10 9 8 7 6 5 4 3 2 1

For Mom and Dad, for everything
—JS

For my sisters
—JW

Journal

STOP READING THIS RIGHT NOW.

IT IS **MY** PERSONAL BUSINESS.

NOT ANYBODY ELSE'S.

That especially means you, Josephine Rosalie Altman. If you turn a single page, I will tell your whole grade that Dad's nickname for you is Bubbles, because you get very gassy.

I AM **NOT** KIDDING, JO.

I AM DEFINITELY NOT.

Dearest Celie,

For my tenth birthday, my father gave me a punching bag and suggested that I slug _it_ instead of slamming doors and hitting my brother. And that is how I became the world-famous boxer I am today.

Okay. As you well know, I am not a world-famous boxer. I am instead a mild-mannered lawyer. However, it was fun having a punching bag, and it did cause at least a small decline in the number of times I hit my brother.

And so today, for your tenth birthday, I present to you a sporty punching bag along with this journal. May you find each beneficial whenever you're struggling to work through your feelings. And may you inflict significantly less violence on Jo. (There are far worse older sisters out there, I promise you.)

All my love,
Dad

This Diary Is the Private Property of

Celie Valentine Altman

Saturday, November 6

It's me, Celie. I cried just now. On my **birthday**.
I was in the kitchen, eating my birthday cake, and
tears started dripping onto my plate. Part of my
cake got soggy. All because of stinking, rotten Lula.

I feel like calling her on the phone and saying
something mean. Like, "I know I said I like that
wheelie thing you use instead of a backpack.
I **lied**. I hate it."

Lula, struggling

Then I'd hang up.

The real truth is, I did
like her wheelie thing.
But now I can't stand it.

Me, moving very freely

LATER, STILL MY BIRTHDAY

Jo helped me with my sadness. Only, not at first. At
first she annoyed me. Because she kept asking why
Lula hadn't come over to celebrate my birthday,
the way she was supposed to.

But I don't **know** why! All I know is, Lula became
a VICIOUS OGRE at the beginning of the
week. For no reason! Then, yesterday, she dropped a
mean note on my desk.

I read that mean note, then ripped it up. But I can't stop my brain from remembering it. It said, "I'm not coming tomorrow. I'm doing something else. Lula."

Why is she doing something else? WHAT MADE HER HATE ME?

I am **not** talking to Jo about this. It was bad enough telling Mom. She kept saying, "I really think I should call Lula's mom and discuss what's happening." I had to make her **promise** not to. Because that would be so **embarrassing!** I'm not a baby.

Jo did help me feel better, though, I have to admit. When she saw how sad I was, and how much I did NOT want to talk about Lula, she left the room for a minute. Then she came back, carrying a long box of foil.

"What are you **doing**?" I said. Because our foil does not tend to leave the kitchen.

"Just trust me," she said.

Then she started gathering up the presents I'd
opened this morning.

"Those are mine!" I said.

"I know that," she said. "Obviously. I'm trying to do
something that will keep you from sitting around
feeling sad on your birthday. Will you please just
trust me?"

So I trusted her. (Except, not with this journal. She
does not get to touch this journal.)

She re-wrapped all of my presents in foil. Then
she hid them around our apartment and wrote
up complicated clues for me. So I could have a
birthday treasure hunt.

Searching for foil-wrapped presents was not exactly
my dream birthday activity. Lula and I were
supposed to rent two movies and watch them both

and eat popcorn AND make ourselves sundaes with whipped cream and hot fudge and chocolate chip cookie crumbs and rainbow sprinkles. Just exactly like we did last year. THOSE were my dream birthday activities.

Still, Jo's treasure hunt was fun. And I do like my presents.

Mom gave me a book of world records. One woman in that book didn't cut her fingernails for 21 **years**! So now she has the world's longest nails. They swoop and curl. It's crazy!

Mom also gave me a sweatshirt that says Narwhals
Are Awesome. Because I love narwhals. I like the
big horn that sticks out of their heads. It's actually
a tooth! It keeps growing and growing out
of their mouths. Like
that woman's nails. Only
the horn is straight.

like this

Dad gave me a
punching bag, which
he's going to hang in my room.
And this great journal. I'm not
just going to write and draw
in here. I'm going to tape
in letters and notes and
report cards—whatever
I can think of. So I can
tell the full story of
my whole life.

not like this

Granny sent me a
white tablecloth with
pretty blue flowers. She

says she got it as a birthday present too, from her mother. Years and years ago. Which is nice. Only, I don't actually need a tablecloth. And she mailed it so early! The package was delivered three weeks ago. I was home with Mom when it came, so I saw it. I could tell it was my birthday present from Granny, because she'd written "Happy Birthday, Sensational Celie!" in her curly handwriting on the outside of the box.

I wanted to open that package right up, but Mom wouldn't let me. She put it in her closet and made me wait until today—my actual birthday.

I don't care about any of that, though. I still love my granny.

Last but not least, Jo gave me a super-official spy notebook. I know **exactly** who I'm going to spy on first. But not until Monday.

BYE!

Even Later,
Still My Birthday

Our housekeeper, Delores, just dropped off homemade zucchini bread for me. And gave me a squishy, perfume-y hug.

I thanked her very much for the bread. It was super nice of her to bring it.

Only, I will not actually be eating it. Because zucchini does not belong in bread. Or anywhere near my stomach.

Jo might eat it, though. She doesn't mind disgusting things.

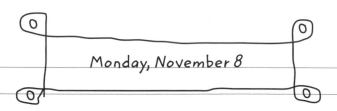

Monday, November 8

At school today I hid my spy notebook inside my Spanish dictionary. And I spied on Lula.

We were supposed to be working on our dialogues in Spanish about our neighborhoods. We work on those dialogues **a lot** in Señora Santacruz's class. Here is my spy report. I cut it so it would fit.

From the
Top Secret Spy Notebook of

Celie Valentine Altman

A spy must never reveal his or her true identity. How are you concealing yours?

I'm not. Every single person in this room definitely knows who I am.

A spy must do his or her best to see and not be seen. How are you trying to be invisible?

I'm in Spanish. I can't be invisible. I can't just vanish from Spanish!

What do you see?

I see the back of Lula's head. She's sitting at the desk in front of me. Her hair is down. Which means she probably tried a ponytail this morning and didn't like it, then tried a headband and didn't like it, then just decided to wear her hair down. She does that a lot.

Now she's looking up something in her Spanish dictionary. Jack B. is leaning over to her and showing her something in his notebook. I can't see what. I bet he wrote FART or PUKE in Spanish.

Now Lula is laughing and laughing. Even though Jack B.'s fart jokes are never funny.

And now Lula just said, way too loudly, "I have to show this to Violet!"

Now she's pulling on Jack B.'s notebook. He obviously doesn't want to give it to her. She shouldn't try to steal other people's notebooks! And she has to stop being so loud!

Shouldn't Señora Santacruz make her be
quiet? She is disturbing everyone!

Spies must hone their powers of
observation or risk missing vital clues.
Pay closer attention! What else do you see?

Lula pulled the notebook away from Jack
B. and stood up with it and walked past me
without even looking at me. Then she showed
the notebook to Violet
and laughed a lot with
Violet and walked back
to her seat without
even looking at me.
Then she sat back
down.

Señora Santacruz did
nothing that whole
time. She didn't even
notice. She should be
fired.

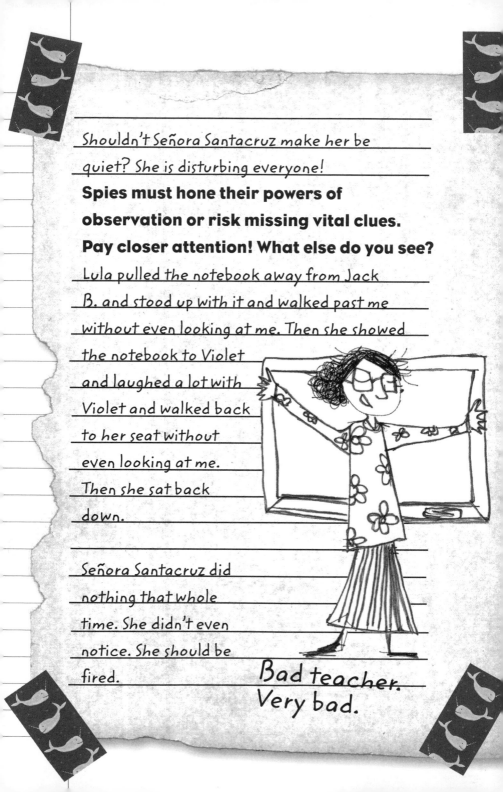

Bad teacher.
Very bad.

I was still cranky about Spanish when Mom picked me up. So she made me stop and draw a million pictures on our walk home. She says drawing helps me get my crank out. And she likes to watch me draw.

Here's my sketch of the snacks we got at the corner store. We both chose our favorites. The black-and-white cookie is mine. Very unfortunately, the icing pulled away from the cookie when I took off the wrapper. That happens sometimes. It is a tragedy. It is also hard to draw:

Terribly tragic cookie

Perfectly normal muffin

Here's a picture of the fire hydrant I almost bumped into, after we left the corner store. Because I was putting the final touches on my muffin-and-cookie drawing, and not paying attention to my walking.

I almost stepped in dog poop, too. But I didn't draw **that.** Yuck!

Here's a picture of
our subway train,
right as it was pulling
into the station:

And here's a sad
picture, about a block
from our building:

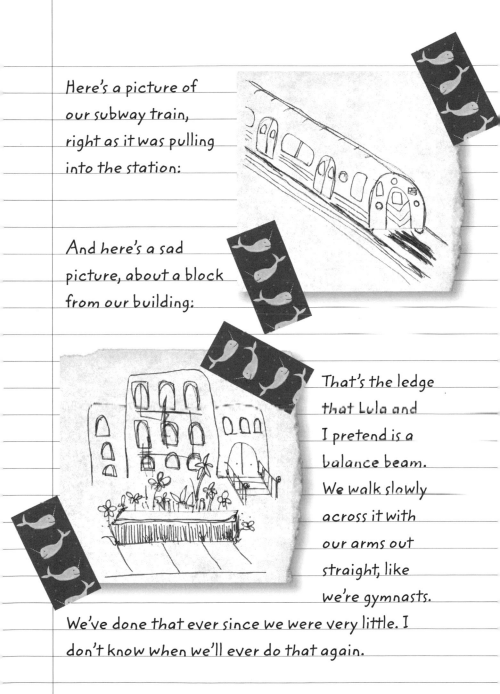

That's the ledge
that Lula and
I pretend is a
balance beam.
We walk slowly
across it with
our arms out
straight, like
we're gymnasts.
We've done that ever since we were very little. I
don't know when we'll ever do that again.

Lula should be very sorry. She doesn't get to walk on the ledge with me, **and** right now Mom is making Granny's famous twice-baked potatoes for dinner. Lula loves those potatoes. I almost want to walk up to her at school tomorrow and tell her. And then say, "Too bad for **you**." And then walk away. Only, I don't actually want to talk to her.

Mom is also making this chicken for dinner:

I feel sorry for raw chicken. It's so germy and funny-looking, and nobody gets close to it. Unless they're about to stick it in a very hot oven.

I liked doing my art walk with Mom. Jo would've had fun too. She would've used the camera on Mom's phone instead of drawing, and she would've taken really interesting pictures. Dad says she has an excellent eye. But she had track after school with her new friend, Trina. Who I do not like **at all**.

Here's one last drawing. Maybe my most favorite one. I made a copy of it on our printer, to send to Granny.

It's a sketch of the painting Granny made me last summer. She was taking a painting class. The teacher told her to paint something small. So she painted a bottle of wart medication.

I didn't really want a painting of wart medication. But Dad said, "Look on the bright side. She could have painted you a wart." Which is a good point. That would have been worse. Plus Jo got a painting of a green pea, which is just boring.

Going to mail Granny's picture to her now.

I AM SO MAD! I've been punching and punching my punching bag.

The punching didn't make me feel better, though. I actually feel worse, because now my hands hurt. Plus they're all red.

Why am I the only one Mom punished? Why wasn't **Jo** sent to our room, too? Or any other room? What she did was so **wrong**! Mom treats Jo a billion times better than she treats me. I'm never talking to either one of them again.

I just realized I've been sitting on one of Jo's dirty socks! **GROSS!! I'VE TOLD HER A MILLION TIMES TO KEEP HER BODY AND ALL HER THINGS OFF MY BED.** And to keep her stuff on **her** side of the dresser! But she leaves it everywhere. Her earrings, and the friendship bracelets she never finishes making, and all those hairbands with broken

strands of her hair. Delores makes everything
so nice and neat, and then in two seconds Jo
MESSES IT ALL UP.

Wait.

I hear noises.

Jo just slid a folded note under the door, into the
room. She wrote my name on the outside—it's
definitely her handwriting.

I am **not** opening that note. She doesn't deserve
for me to read it. I don't want to know what she has
to say. I'm going to push all her stuff off the dresser
now.

Bye.

LATER, SAME DAY

I'm back. I didn't push Jo's stuff onto the floor. I
put it on her bed instead. Plus her dirty sock. Then I
read her stupid note:

Dear Celie,

Mom says I'm not allowed to talk to you (I'm supposed to "give you your space") until the end of your timeout, so I can't just go in there and tell you this, which is what I really want to do.

The thing is, I totally didn't mean to read that letter from Mrs. McElhaney. I was just looking through your backpack for a pencil with an eraser that works, because I couldn't find one anywhere else. You didn't have any in the front pocket of your backpack, so I started digging through the main pocket and that's when I saw it. The letter, I mean. Scrunched up in front of your homework folder.

It looked like garbage all scrunched up like that, so I guess I figured it wouldn't matter if I took it out and started reading. So that's what I did. I hadn't read very far at all before you grabbed it away and kicked me. OW! Did you have to kick so hard? I'm going to have one of those yellow and blue bruises that remind me of Granny's bathroom counters, I can already tell.

I'll forgive you, though, if you slide a note back saying you forgive me, too.

Love,
Jo

P.S. Do you want to talk to me about what happened? I'm guessing it has something to do with Lula, and I really do think I could be a big help. Not to brag or anything, but I'm excellent at friends stuff. xo

What a **stupid** note! Every single part of it is stupid. I wish I hadn't read it.

She thinks she's so smart, but she's not! She's a sixth grader, not a grown-up! Plus she's **not at all** excellent at friends stuff. Look at her new best friend—**Trina**. Always rolling her eyes and smacking her gum and telling Jo secrets right in front of me. Even though everybody knows that secrets aren't nice.

And also, Jo chews pencil erasers! That's why she couldn't find one that worked! She is disgusting.

I don't have to tell her everything about my life. She does **not** need to know what my teachers say about me. I don't know what her teachers say about **her**.

I am not answering her. That's all I have to say.

LATER, SAME DAY

I didn't write Jo back, but she cannot take a hint.
She just slid **this** under the door:

Dear Celie,

I can't believe I forgot to say this in my other note! I still
have part of the Mrs. McElhaney letter—which, by the way, never
would've ripped in the first place if you'd just asked me for it nicely
instead of grabbing it.

Anyway, don't worry, I can't tell anything from the words
I have on my piece. And I won't try to put it back in your backpack
because I know you, and I am positive you don't want me going
anywhere near your backpack right now, or probably ever. I'll just
paperclip the ripped-off piece of the letter to this note and slide the
whole thing under the door.

I'm going to knock, too, so you'll know to look toward the door.
My other note should also be there. I think you might've missed it.

Lots of love,

Jo

P.S. Something weird's going on with Mom. When I just
walked into her office, she was reading her email, and she definitely
said out loud, "What in the world?!" in a shocked voice. So I said,
"What is it? What happened?" And she said, "Nothing," really fast—
which was so clearly not true. So I said, "No, really, tell me!" And she
got all mad and said, "Can I have a little privacy, please? Please?"
So I had to leave. Too bad you can't come out here and spy on her and
figure it all out.

I'm curious about Mom now. I want to go spy. But I am **not** telling Jo that.

She's been knocking and knocking ever since she slid that note under the door. Like I'm an idiot. So I'm writing her back. I'm going to tell her:

Stop knocking! I see your notes. I'm **ignoring** you.

Still the same day

Here's the ripped letter from Mrs. McElhaney. Mom's already read it. And I can't think of anywhere else to keep it private.

❀ FROM THE DESK OF VICKY McELHANEY ❀

FOURTH GRADE TEACHER

Dear Mrs. Altman,

I'm afraid Celie and Lula had another tough day today. It's hard to see them struggle! Celie in particular has now begun to withdraw in a way that I fear could interfere with her learning. Fortunately, as I mentioned earlier, the Friendship Forward program is tailor-made for these types of difficulties.

I've now explained the program to both girls and arranged for them to start this week. They'll meet with school counselor Rebecca Wilde during recess once or twice a week, beginning Friday. She might also give them a few assignments.

Many of my fourth graders have benefited from Friendship Forward. I'm confident Celie and Lula will as well.

Please let me know if you have any questions.

With all best wishes,

V.M.

I don't like what she said about my learning. There is nothing wrong with my learning. And I definitely don't want to go to Friendship Forward. Last year when Billy and Sasha went, everybody knew and everybody talked about it.

I don't want everybody talking about me. Trying to figure out what's the matter with me. Plus Billy and Sasha went because Billy spat on Sasha and Sasha punched Billy's ear one day during recess. I didn't punch or spit on anybody. I'm not even being mean. Lula should have to go by herself.

I told Mom I'm not going. But she said I have to. **And** she started talking **again** about calling Lula's mom.

"You and Lula have been so close for so long," she said. "It's a special relationship. Don't you want me to help you protect it?"

I was so **mad** then. I told her, **"Stop!"** Then

I shoved the note back in my backpack and stomped down the hall.

Only, that turned out to be stupid. Because Jo found the note scrunched up in there. And now I'm stuck in the LONGEST TIMEOUT IN THE HISTORY OF THE WORLD.

Same Day. Of course.

I'm bored bored bored bored bored. Boy am I bored.

And also, starving!

Isn't it time for dinner? Is Mom not going to feed me? Plus, doesn't she know I have homework in my backpack out there? I'm going to FAIL OUT OF SCHOOL and DIE OF STARVATION, and it will be all her fault.

Wait—more noises.

x

And, yes, **another** note from Jo:

If you want to ignore me so badly, then fine, go ahead. But remember last week, when you were trying to make an old T-shirt into a walrus? Remember—you dropped your needle on the rug and I stepped on it? I didn't ignore you when you apologized! After the terrible pain had gone away and Mom had vacuumed so I wouldn't have to be afraid walking barefoot in my own home, and then Delores had vacuumed some more, I forgave you.

Anyway. I just peeked into the office, and Mom is lying on her back, on the wooden floor by her desk, with her hands over her eyes. Isn't that so weird? I said, "Mom? Are you okay?" And without even taking her hands off her eyes she said, "I'm fine, thanks." And I said, "Why are you lying on the floor?" And she said—still with her hands over her eyes!—"I'm not entirely sure. It feels good though." And I said, "Do you need help?" And she said, "Just a little peace and quiet, please. That would be a big help."

So I'm giving her peace and quiet. But I've got nothing to do out here. And you're still mad at me, and Mom has gone bonkers. Today sucks.

Jo

Now I'm a little worried about Mom. And also, it sounds like she's forgotten all about dinner.

SAME DAY, STILL NO DINNER.

I just tried lying on the floor with my hands over my eyes. It did not feel good. It felt uncomfortable. But I did have a genius idea while I was lying there. I got up and wrote to Jo. I drew on that note, too. It looked just like this.

Jo—

You know your art supply set? I will forgive you if you give me the sketching pencils that smell like the forest. And if you promise to never read anything that belongs to me ever again.

Celie

Because I love those yummy-smelling pencils.
And also, being mad is tiring.

FINALLY!

I am eating a banana. Because Mom finally opened
the door, and I am free!

Still no dinner, though. Mom says she's working on it.

I kind of want to smudge some of my banana here,
so I'll have it forever. Because it is my Fruit of
Freedom! Only, that would be disgusting.

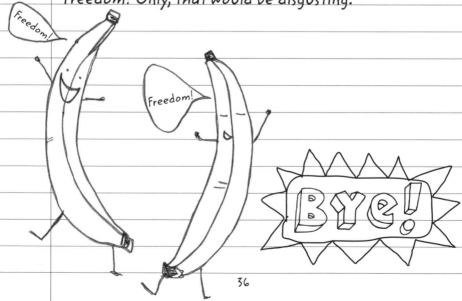

November 9 again, but late at night

I'm deep under my covers now, with a flashlight.
Mom and Dad turned off our lights a while ago. Jo
fell asleep right away, but not me. I couldn't sleep at
all. And I could hear Mom and Dad's voices in the
living room. So I decided to do some spying.

I tiptoed down the hall very quietly. And I sat close
to the bathroom door. So I could pretend I had to
pee, if I heard Mom or Dad coming.

Here's my spy report:

From the
Top-Secret Spy Notebook of
Celie Valentine Altman
Remember: Spies must be alert at all times!
Practice using each of your senses. Answer
each of these questions in the space below:

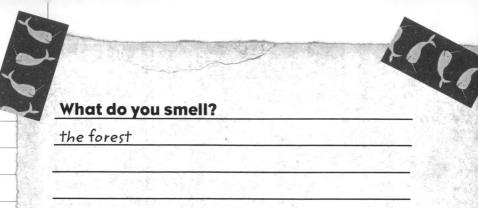

What do you smell?

the forest

What do you taste?

Spit? Air? I don't know! I'm not eating anything!

What do you see?

white wall

crack in wall paint, coming down from ceiling

wood floor

hairband with Jo's hair on floor

What do you feel?

Annoyed. Jo's hairbands and hairs are

everywhere!

What do you hear?

Mom and Dad's voices

(voices too quiet—I'm scooching closer)

Mom's saying: Now it's just sitting over Baton

Rouge. I hate thinking of her all alone in that big house with a storm raging outside. I've only watched a little of the coverage. I didn't want the girls to see it and worry. It upsets me, too. There's so little I can do from here.

Dad: Have you tried calling?

Mom: I keep getting a busy signal. The phone lines must be down. I begged her to go stay with Meepsie, but she flat-out refused.

Dad: Who can blame her? I would refuse to stay with Meepsie. Wouldn't you?

Mom: I know, but this is an emergency.

Dad: It's not an emergency yet.

Mom: I wish the Weavers hadn't moved.

Dad: Your mom's survived these storms plenty of times before.

Mom: But remember when we saw her in September? How much slower she was moving? She is seventy-five. And that email from Meepsie today! That was so disturbing! Do you think Mom's mind is slipping?

Dad: I don't think so. But let me take another look at the email.

Mom: Hold on a second.

(both of them are quiet)

(still quiet)

Mom: It's not connecting.

(quiet again)

Mom: Ugh. What a day! Nothing is going right. Do you think it's the router?

Dad: I'll check.

I heard footsteps then, so I had to stop writing. I **ran** into the bathroom and shut the door. **One second later** Dad knocked and said, "Who's that in there?"

"Celie!" I said. "I'm peeing!" Which was sort of a lie. I was still on my way to the toilet.

He said, through the door, "Pee away! Then straight back to bed with you."

I tried to pee, but I couldn't get anything out. Now I'm back in bed. And I want to know if something's wrong with Granny! I'm worried! What if the storm knocks a tree on top of her? What if she's too slow to get away? And what did Mom mean about a slipping mind? WHAT IS IN MEEPSIE'S EMAIL?

Granny's not **that** slow, though. There are lots of slower old ladies. Like the one I got stuck behind on the subway steps yesterday. Granny's **much** faster than that woman.

I have to talk to Jo about all this. Going to wake her up now.

Even Later

Jo made me feel better. I closed our door very quietly and shook her awake. She opened her eyes wide. When she saw me, she sat up fast. "What time is it?" she said. "What happened? What's wrong?"

I sat beside her and told her the whole story in a whisper.

She put her arm around me then. And she said, "I think everything's going to be fine, I really do. Mom and Dad are just worriers. They won't even let me go by myself to the drugstore around the corner, right? Every other sixth grader I know gets to do that. Every single one. So you have to remember, our parents worry."

I nodded. That made sense.

"Want to crawl in bed with me?" Jo asked.

I kind of wanted to. But I shook my head. Because there is not a lot of room in Jo's bed with Jo in it. And I knew I wouldn't sleep.

"You could turn on a book light and write in your journal instead, if you want," Jo said. "I won't mind."

So that's what I've been doing. And it has helped me.

But now I'm very tired. It's time to turn off the light.

Good night.

Wednesday, November 10, just after school

I hate this whole day.

Before school Mom tried to call Granny. But her phone was still busy.

At least Mom reached Meepsie. And Meepsie said Granny's house didn't look too damaged, just some tree branches down. She promised to check on Granny this morning. So that wasn't too terrible.

But then, in math, Nora sent me this note:

Celie,

Want to go with me and Gracie to Lula's movie party on Friday? If you want to, I'll tell my mom to ask your mom.
Your friend,

Nora

I felt so bad, reading that note. I didn't even know
Lula was having a party. So she obviously didn't
invite me.

I told Nora I wasn't going. Then I did something
very stupid. I asked her who else was invited. She
said Violet and Hannah and Isabel and Gracie and
Blythe and Chloe and Elle. Practically the whole
universe! Except for me.

Plus, Nora said Lula is renting two movies for that
party. JUST LIKE my birthday celebration
that got cancelled because of LULA'S
MEANNESS! That is <u>evil</u>.

Maybe I could sneak
into Lula's house in the
middle of thenight and
cut off all her hair.

At least my day
got better in
science. Because
Mrs. McElhaney told us our
assignments for our animal
reports. And I got sloths! I really wanted sloths.
They are SO SLOW. And furry. And they sleep
ALL THE TIME. Hanging upside down in trees!

When Mrs. McElhaney was about to tell Lula
her animal, I sent strong brain waves to Mrs.
McElhaney, saying, "COCKROACHES!
GIVE LULA COCKROACHES! She has
dead cockroaches sometimes in her building's
basement! So that is the perfect subject for her!"

But Mrs. McElhaney did not receive my waves. She
gave Lula otters. Which are obviously better than

cockroaches. But still, not nearly as good as sloths.

Then the day got bad again. Because after lunch
I saw Jo in the hallway with her friend Trina. And
Jo said Trina's coming over this afternoon, after
they finish track. Which means they'll be home any
minute. But I hate Trina! Jo knows I hate Trina!
She should STOP inviting her over! She should
stop being Trina's friend at all. They never used to be
friends, until Jo joined the track team. I hate that
stupid team.

I want to go fall asleep upside down in a tree now.
Like a sloth. Hidden in the branches.

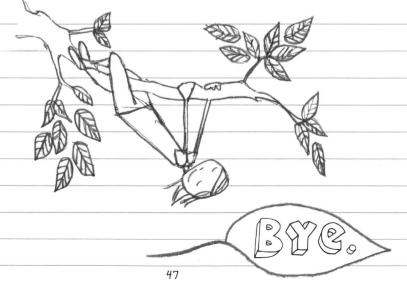

Bye.

Now I hate today even more! Jo and Trina came home from track. They ate popcorn for snack and left kernels and salty white crumbs all over the sofa. I **told** them we're supposed to eat in the kitchen. But Trina said, in a really annoying voice, "Relax. God. You're so uptight." And Jo **laughed**! Then they walked away from me, down the hall. AND THEN THEY LOCKED ME OUT OF MY OWN ROOM!

I banged and banged on that door. I shouted at Jo, too. I shouted things like: "**OPEN THIS DOOR RIGHT NOW!** It's my room too. You're **NEVER** allowed to lock the door. You and Trina **HAVE** to let me in!"

And Jo shouted back stupid things like: "We just want a little privacy. Can't we have a little privacy? **YOU HAVE THE WHOLE LIVING ROOM AND WHOLE KITCHEN AND BOTH BATHROOMS TO YOURSELF!**"

I couldn't BELIEVE that. I said: "YOU WANT ME TO PLAY IN THE BATHROOMS? I am telling Mom NOW!"

Right away I went to tell Mom. But she was in her bedroom with HER DOOR LOCKED. She NEVER locks the door! So I banged on her door, too, and shouted at her, too.

She cracked open her door and said, "I am on a very important call. I will be with you in a few minutes. For now, though, I need you to leave me be, unless you are having a true medical emergency. Do you need to go to the hospital?"

I had to say no. Because I didn't actually need the hospital.

"Fine," she said. "I'll be out in a bit."

And then she locked me out AGAIN!

That was the first time in my life I ever wished I was having a true medical emergency.

I shouted at her, "DO YOU WANT ME TO PLAY IN THE BATHROOMS? WITH ALL THE GERMS?" But she ignored me.

Then I thought about what she'd said. About a very important call. What could that be, except for a call about Granny?

Then I got even madder. Because everybody excluded me from everything! It wasn't fair.

So I went right into Mom's office and right over to her computer and right into her email. And I found Meepsie's email about Granny.

I'm not supposed to go on Mom's computer, because her author work is on it. But Mom didn't stop Jo from getting kernels all over the sofa or from locking me out. So why shouldn't I break rules, too?

What a scary email Meepsie sent! I printed it out.
The printer was ridiculously loud! Line after line
of beeps and rattling. I worried the whole time
that Mom would hear and come see what was
happening. But she didn't.

Here's the email. I had to tape it in sideways so it
would fit:

from   **Meepsie Dixon** mdixon@pipingmail.com
to   Elizabeth Altman <ealtman@xenithmail.com>
date   Tuesday, November 9, 3:59 PM
subject   your mama's freezer

Lizzie, I just got back from your mama's house. I stopped by to remind her that I'm right next door, happy to have her if she doesn't want to be all by her lonesome during the storm. She declined—you know how stubborn your mama is. Anyhoo, I stayed to chat. I was just getting myself some ice for my Diet Coke, thinking about how you and I used to ride our bikes together to the 7-11 for Big Gulps—weren't those drinks humungous!—when I couldn't help but notice that your mama is storing a bag of trash in her freezer. A clear kitchen trash bag, tied in a knot at the top. I saw rubber gloves in there and old roach motels, even a couple of pink sponge curlers. I would hope that not a living soul is using those uncomfortable curlers any more. At any rate I came back out of the kitchen and I said to your mama, "Miss Arlene, do you need help getting rid of your trash?" And she said, "I don't need help with anything, thank you very much, Meepsie." And I said, "Are you sure?" And she said, "Actually, I've just realized I have to send you on your way now. I have an urgent need for a bath." "A <u>bath</u>?" I said. "Before you've even had supper?" And she said, "Yes, dear." Then she shoved me to the door, without even giving me a chance to finish my Diet Coke. Which is, of course, beside the point. The point is, Lizzie: Why is your mama freezing her trash?

I hate to add to your burden—you with your work and your busy husband, and your two gorgeous children. I just thought you ought to know.

Yours truly,
Meepsie

This is what I thought when I read that email: I thought, I don't like Meepsie. Her hands are sweaty and she laughs too loud. But she is not a liar. So,

WHY IS GRANNY FREEZING HER TRASH?

And then I thought, I need to talk to Jo right now.

And then I thought, I **hate** Stupid Trina! Because Trina was still locked in my room with Jo. And there was NO WAY I was risking Mean-a Trina seeing that email about Granny.

So I sat on the hallway floor outside the room, and I waited.

I drew a big picture of Mean-a Trina.

Then I scooched close to our bedroom door and tried to listen through it, to what Jo and Trina were saying. I couldn't hear everything. But I definitely heard the word "bra." And the word "period." And the word "kiss." Which all made me feel VERY uncomfortable.

I moved back away from the door and thought instead about the problems I'd like Trina to have. Like diarrhea. And lice.

Only, I shouldn't have thought about lice. Because my whole head started to itch. Then my neck. Then my back.

I couldn't just sit there, itching. So I got up and started knocking on our bedroom door.

Jo hollered at me to go away.

I kept knocking.

"You're giving me a headache!" Trina shouted.

Jo opened the door a little and said to me, "Please, please, please stop being so embarrassing."

"I have to show you something!" I told her. "It's important!"

She looked very serious.

"If I let you come in and show me," she said, "will you stop bothering us?"

"Yes, I will," I said. So she let me in.

Right away I saw Trina, sitting on our rug and smacking her gum. Way too close to my bed.

"You have to get in the closet," I told her. "And close the door."

"Celie!" Jo cried.

"She can't see what I have to show you!" I said.

"She's not going in the closet!" Jo said. "If she can't see whatever it is, then just leave the room and show me after she's gone home."

I didn't want to leave the room, or wait that long. I did some fast thinking.

"Fine," I said. "Then she has to swear an oath in **writing** that she won't tell anyone. Ever. And she has to swear on something that **really matters**. Like her life."

Trina rolled her eyes. Then she ripped a piece of paper out of the notebook on the floor beside her and wrote this:

i, Trina Walker, swear on my collection of skinny jeans that i will not tell anyone whatever it is Celie is talking about

I could not believe that pathetic oath!

"SKINNY JEANS?!" I said, as soon as I'd read it. "Skinny jeans don't matter! They're **pants**! And also, it has to be a blood oath. I'll find you something to cut yourself with."

I was ready to get a big knife from the kitchen. But

Jo stopped me. And told me I was being ridiculous.
And put her hands on her hips and said I should stop
being so rude and show both of them what I had or
just LEAVE THEM ALONE.

"But it has to do with Granny," I told her.

"Granny's fine—her phone's back up, and the storm
wasn't that bad," Jo said. "Mom already told me."

"That's not what I mean," I said.

"Is this the same Granny
who did the wart painting?"
Trina said. She started to
laugh. "That painting is
hilarious."

"It's not a wart," I told her. "It's wart
medication."

Then I stomped out of that room. Because there
was NO WAY I was telling Skinny Jeans

anything about Granny.

Jo called after me, but I didn't turn back or stop. Not even for a second. She should've left Trina and followed me. And apologized for picking Trina over me. Then I probably would've shown her the email.

But she didn't. She just let me leave. So now she's lost her chance forever.

Later. Sitting in Living room. All alone.

Mom hasn't checked on me and neither has Jo. I'm not talking to either one of them ever again.

I wish Dad was home.

I don't care what Skinny Jeans or anybody else says.

I love Granny's paintings.

I want to take a bath, before I've even had supper.
Just like Granny.

NOTES FROM THE TUB

Granny is the only person in the world who would use
wart medication for art. Nobody else would ever
think of that.

She is original and creative.

So maybe she's using frozen trash for art, too?
Original and creative art?

Maybe.

I wish I could try using frozen trash for art. Only,
I don't want to touch trash. Especially right now,
because this bath has made me very clean.

Like Granny would say, I'm fresh as a daisy!

Ta-da! My beautiful picture of a real-life frozen
dryer sheet that came straight from the trash!

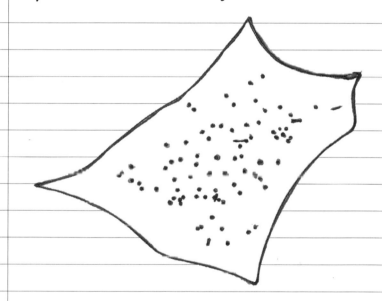

I am very proud of myself. I used a napkin to lift
that dryer sheet out of our kitchen garbage after
my bath yesterday. The dryer sheet was pretty
wet—I think milk got on it in the trash. Also,
some coffee grounds got on it. Which is a tiny bit
disgusting. But very artistic and interesting.

Anyway, I hid the sheet in the back of the freezer. It stayed there all night.

Now it is very frozen. And very beautiful. I'm going to clear out a whole desk drawer for it. So it's a little hidden, and doesn't get crushed.

Here's another picture, from a different angle:

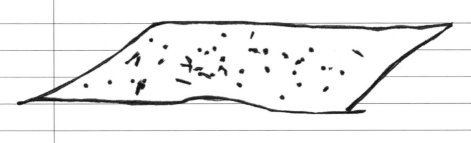

I wish it would never melt.

Friday, November 12

Friendship Forward started today.

It was terrible.

I should've fake-fainted, so I wouldn't have had to go.

It was so **awkward**, there in Miss Wilde's dark office. Lula sat as far from me as she possibly could on the leather couch. Plus I don't think she looked at me once. Whenever I peeked at her, she was staring right at Miss Wilde. And she sat so straight, with her hands folded in her lap. Like she was just perfect. So I had to sit all stiff and tall, too. Which gave me a big backache.

Miss Wilde sat across from us, in a wooden chair. **She** didn't look stiff. She looked pretty. I like her dark hair. But she waited too long whenever it was her turn to say something. She squinted and nodded, when she should have been talking. I kept wanting to tell her, "Stop **nodding!** Start *talking!*"

She did ask us a bunch of questions. Not hard ones. Just whether we liked school, and how long we had known each other, and had we always been in the same classes. Stuff like that.

I didn't say much. Lula didn't say much either.

Then Miss Wilde gave us our writing assignment. Basically, she told us to write a letter to each other.

"A letter about what's happened between you," she said, tilting her head and squinting at both of us. "Because it can be easier to write about our feelings than to talk about them." She put her hand on her heart. "Please be **very honest** about your feelings."

Also, she said, "Don't worry about your friend reading it. I promise not to show her, or anyone."

"Wait," I said. "I'm writing a letter to Lula that Lula isn't going to read? Shouldn't I just write a letter to you?"

"I love that question," Miss Wilde said, nodding even more than usual. "Writing to Lula will help you tap into your feelings about Lula. Does that make sense?"

Before I could decide whether or not it made sense, Lula spoke up.

"I want to start," she said. "Can I have some paper, please?"

Miss Wilde handed Lula a sheet of paper, and Lula turned her whole body away from me. So I could only see her ponytail and the back of her purple sweater. Then she leaned over to the coffee table in front of the couch and started to write and write and write.

I couldn't believe it! What was she writing? So much and so fast!

I stopped watching her and stuck my hand out

toward Miss Wilde.

"Me too," I said. Super mad. "I want to write about **my** feelings, too. Right now."

Miss Wilde handed me a few sheets of paper. I leaned over to the coffee table and wrote this letter:

~~Dear~~ To Lula,

    I feel like pushing you off this couch. That is the honest truth about my feelings. Why are you being so mean to me? I never did a **single thing** wrong.

    Not Your Friend Anymore,

            Celie

Lula was still writing when I finished. Writing and writing.

I didn't like that **at all**. She couldn't possibly be telling the truth! If she was telling the truth, she wouldn't want Miss Wilde to know.

I decided **I'd** better tell the whole truth. Because Lula was probably blaming me. Unfairly! I took a second sheet of paper and wrote:

To Lula,

I'm supposed to write what happened between us. Only, I don't know what happened between us!

We were best friends. We'd been best friends FOREVER. We never used to fight. I pulled out your first loose tooth for you, because you were scared it would hurt. I got my stuffed hippo Shanghai to match your stuffed hippo Beijing. SHANGHAI IS VERY MAD AT YOU! I know that you actually love that singer that you tell everyone else you hate. I never told a single soul. I'm not even writing his name now, because Miss Wilde will read this. THAT IS HOW GOOD I AM AT KEEPING YOUR SECRETS!

Then we had that play date at your house, when that thing happened with your parents that I am also not going to talk about because you asked me not to tell anyone. I am **STILL KEEPING YOUR SECRETS.** Then, all of a sudden, you stopped talking to me. You wouldn't be my partner in math or Spanish anymore. And you asked Mrs. McElhaney to change your table so you don't sit with me during Words, Words, Words anymore. And you said I wasn't allowed to hang out with you and Violet during recess.

When Mrs. McElhaney saw how upset I was about recess, she said you weren't allowed to say I wasn't allowed. But it didn't matter. I'm not going to go anywhere near you and Violet—because you are ALWAYS with Violet now—if you don't want me to. I'll be with Nora. _She's_ a nice person.

I want to read that letter you're writing over there. I hate it that I can't. It's a letter to _me_! I should be able to read it!

That's as far as I got before Miss Wilde collected
our papers. She read them quickly, her face very
serious. Then she handed them back.

"These letters are for you," she said. "They are an
important part of the process."

The bell rang then. Lula and I both stood up. I
refused to look at her. I will never look at her again.

"I want you both to dig deep this weekend," Miss
Wilde told me and Lula, as she opened the door for
us to leave. "Really dig deep. Try to think about this
from the other person's point of view. That is your
homework assignment. I'll see you next week."

That is the weirdest homework assignment ever.
I know one thing for sure. I know Lula is not digging
deep right now. She's having her big movie party,
with everyone else but me.

Maybe Coke will get spilled in her lap.

I want chocolate pudding.

Later

Delores was here, and she made her famous double chocolate fudge brownies! They were even better than pudding!

I love Delores.

delicious yummy goodness, by Delores

A Little Later

Sometimes Delores straightens things a little too much. Jo just found this note from Dad, to me and Jo, in a stack of papers on the kitchen table:

Dearest Daughters,

　　　I forgot to tell you something before you both ran out the door after your mother, screaming at one another: "You always make me late for school!" "I never make you late for school!" "Call the elevator!" "Where are you going?! WHY ARE YOU TAKING OFF YOUR SHIRT?" "It has water on it." "It will DRY!! DAD! TELL CELIE SHE CAN'T CHANGE HER SHIRT! WE DON'T HAVE TIME!!!"

　　　Wouldn't it be fun, just once, to depart calmly and quietly, like little ducklings waddling in a row behind the Mama Duck? Shall we try it on Monday? I'll waddle with you, all the way to the elevator.

　　　And now, here is the news I forgot to share: I will be home early tonight, and we will all have dinner and a family meeting. I will come bearing dessert and libations. Celie, you are in charge of those ice cubes in which you have been known to freeze large chunks of fruit. Bubbles, I have four words for you: egg in a hole.

　　　And now it is late. I must run screaming through the house without changing my shirt and call the elevator.

　　　Never forget how much I love you both.

　　　　　　　　　xoxoxoxox,
　　　　　　　　　Dad

A family meeting! I wonder why. Are we in trouble?
Did something happen? Is it about Granny?

I bet it **is** about Granny. Mom and Dad must be
worried about Meepsie's email. I guess they don't
realize yet—I have to tell them that the frozen
trash is most probably art. They'll feel better then.

Only, I'm not supposed to know about the frozen
trash.

Today is so HARD!

Later

We're waiting for Dad now. He's on his way, but stuck
in traffic.

Jo just finished eggs in a hole that look like this.
I am **not** eating the burnt one.

Jo cooked me way too long!

And here's a picture of our table, which I set with Granny's pretty tablecloth. The one she gave me for my birthday:

I have to go check on my ice cubes. I hope they had enough time to freeze.

AFTER DINNER, SAME DAY

I hated that dinner. My ice cubes melted in two seconds and Jo dripped yolk on Granny's pretty tablecloth. We might never get that stain out. Plus Mom and Dad had stinking, rotten news.

Practically as soon as we sat down, Jo said, "So why are we having this family meeting?"

Mom looked at Dad, who looked back at her. Then she set her fork down.

"I don't want you girls to get frightened when I say this," she said.

Which made me very frightened! My stomach did a flip, and I put my own fork down.

"I have to go away for a week or two," she said.

"Does this have to do with Granny?" I said.

Mom nodded.

I tried to figure out very fast how to ask about the Meepsie email without showing that I knew about the Meepsie email. But it was hard.

"You already told me that Granny's fine," Jo said to Mom then. "You said the storm didn't hit her house very hard. Remember?"

"Yes," Mom said. "But this isn't about the storm."

Oh no! I thought. They really believe Granny is crazy!

"Granny does **art**," I said, trying to explain. I started miming someone painting. "She's very **creative**."

Everyone stared at me like I was crazy.

"What does that have to do with anything?" Jo said.

"Never mind," I said. My mind start spinning again, trying to figure out what to say.

"Granny is getting older," Mom said. "She might be having some health issues. We're not sure. I want to check it out and make sure everything's being done that needs to be done."

"Granny is fine," I said. "Her body AND HER MIND are fine."

Mom and Dad really focused on me then.

"Why would you mention her mind?" Dad said. "Has she said something strange to you on the phone? Or in her letters?"

"Not at **all**," I said, very fast. I was so mad at myself! I should never have mentioned her mind! "She's FINE."

They didn't stop looking worried.

"I've spoken to Granny," Mom said. "We're just going to have her doctors run some tests. I'd like to be there with her for that."

My heart fell fast then. Because why did Granny agree to tests, if nothing really was wrong with her?

And then I realized **another** problem.

"Who's going to take care of us?" I said. "While you're gone and Dad's at work?"

Mom and Dad looked at each other.

Then Dad said, "Cousin Carla."

"WHAT?" Jo practically shouted.

"We don't like Cousin Carla!" I said. "She's **embarrassing!**"

"Her jeans come down too low!" Jo said. "And so do her V-necks! She shows too many cracks!"

"Oh, dear," Dad said.

"You've never complained about the older girls in your school who show their cracks," Mom said to Jo.

"Can we please stop talking about cracks?" Dad said.

"Cousin Carla is too old to show cracks!" I said, ignoring him.

"Forty is not old," Dad said. "Life starts at forty."

"Wrinkles start at forty," Jo said. "Squishiness starts at forty."

"I'm suddenly feeling self-conscious," Mom said.

"No more talk of aging," Dad said. "What matters is that Cousin Carla is a nice person, regardless of her choice of clothing. And she's not working right now, so she can pick you up at school and bring you here and take care of you until I get home from work."

"What about Delores?" I said. "Delores would be so much better."

"Delores has other jobs," Mom said. "She's only available one morning a week."

"Cousin Carla is NOT picking me up from school," Jo said. "I'm old enough to go on the subway by myself. Everybody else goes home alone—Trina and Michaela and Caroline have been doing it since last year."

"I'm going home with Jo," I said. "Just the two of us."

Both my parents were shaking their heads.

"You're not ready for that," Mom said.

"WE'RE not ready for that," Dad said.

"Cousin Carla will do a good job taking care of you," Mom said.

"I don't need taking care of!" Jo said.

"We all need taking care of," Dad said.

Jo ignored him.

"When exactly are you leaving?" she said to Mom. "Because Trina's supposed to come over Monday afternoon. We've been planning it forever."

"I'm leaving Sunday," Mom said. "But there's no reason Trina can't come over. It will be perfectly fine with Cousin Carla."

"Or maybe it won't be fine," I said. Because I hate Trina.

Jo glared at Mom.

"Unless you tell me right now that you trust me enough to go home without a grown-up and wait for Dad on my own, like a sixth grader—which I *am*," she said, "—then I'm not talking to you anymore."

She glared at Dad, too.

"Or you," she said.

"I'm sorry," Mom said. "But we can't tell you that."

Jo stood up then, with her mouth closed really tight, and left the room. I stood up, too, and followed her into our room. I wanted to start writing this right away.

And that was how that suckish dinner ended.

Date and time:

Saturday, November 13, 11:13 AM

Remember: Know the enemy! Collect information on his or her misdeeds, past and/or present. Interview possible witnesses. Paste any evidence gathered here.

Misdeed #1: One day last month, Jo and I were reading happily on the sofa in our living room. AND THEN Cousin Carla plopped herself down between us. "Time for girl talk!" she said. And I thought, Uh-oh. Then Cousin Carla said to Jo, "So. When I was your age, I got my period."

The second she said "period," I buried my head under a big throw pillow. But she kept going.

"I walked around with toilet paper in my pants," she said, "because I couldn't stand the thought of telling my mom. I want you both to know that you do **not** have to walk around with toilet paper in your pants. You come talk to me. I'll take care of you. Got it?"

I did not look out from under that pillow. I heard Jo say, "Um . . . thanks." Then I felt her get off the couch.

So I threw the pillow off the couch and jumped up too. "I need fruit!" I said, without even looking at Cousin Carla. And I ran out of the room.

Misdeed #2: One day over the summer, while Mom and Dad were both at one of Dad's lawyer conferences, Cousin Carla took me to Lula's for a play date. She was supposed to just drop me off. **Instead**, she came inside Lula's apartment with me. And stayed **forever**. She told Lula and me and Lula's mom a RIDICULOUSLY LONG story about a cab driver. And then she called that guy two bad words! Very bad words that I definitely cannot say! I wanted to close myself in the refrigerator. I **know** Lula's mom didn't like it. She covered Lula's ears. And Cousin Carla just said, "Oops."

Misdeed #3: Aren't those two enough??? How could Mom and Dad **ever** leave us with that **embarrassing** person?

I just had a call with Granny.

It was not good.

I called to tell her that I'd used her pretty tablecloth. And also, to ask how she was feeling.

I decided **not** to tell her about Jo's egg yolk stain.

I used the phone in Mom's office. Since it was quiet in there.

Granny answered after a few rings.

"Hello?" she said.

And I said, "Hey! It's me! Celie!"

There was a long pause. I knew Granny was on the line. I could hear her raspy breathing. But she didn't say a single word.

I was about to ask if she was okay. But then, in a quiet voice, she spoke.

"Ava?" she said.

Then I didn't say anything. I didn't know what to say! I'd just told her I was Celie. Who was Ava?

"Granny?" I said finally. "It's <u>Celie</u>. Can you hear me? Is your phone working?"

Again, there was a long pause. Then Granny laughed a little. I was so relieved to hear her rattly laugh.

"Celie!" she said. "Marvelous Celie. I got confused, didn't I? How strange. Let's start over. Tell me how my beautiful granddaughter is doing."

We had a normal conversation after that. Until I

said, "Granny? Who's Ava?" And she said, "Well, Ava was my older sister. My sweet older sister. She died long before you were born. It turned out she had a weak heart."

I felt very cold then. Because why would Granny think Ava was calling? If Ava was **dead**?

I couldn't say to Granny, "You know that dead people don't use the phone, right?"

So instead I said, "I love you, Granny."

And she said, "I love you too, sweetheart."

And then we hung up.

Later

The more I thought about Ava, the more scared I got.

Mostly for Granny. Because probably something was

going wrong in her head. Probably the frozen trash wasn't just art.

I also got a tiny bit scared for **me**. Because in my mind I kept seeing a very old dead woman climbing out of her grave to make phone calls. It was creepy.

I found Mom in her room, packing. I sat next to some piles of clothes on her bed. And I told her about Ava.

Mom's face got very worried. She moved the piles of clothes and sat beside me.

"I wish I could tell you that I know exactly what is happening with Granny," she said. "But I don't know."

"Will the doctors be able to fix her?" I asked.

"I hope so," she said. But I could see what she was really thinking. I could see that she was thinking, "Probably not."

I felt my eyes fill up then.

Mom put her arm around me.

"You listen to me," she said. "Life has lots of stages. And all those stages have pluses and minuses. Think about babies. Everyone wants to hold them and hug them. But babies can't talk to anyone. Pluses and minuses. Right?"

"I guess," I said.

"It's possible Granny's moving into a new stage," Mom said. "But if she is, we'll find the pluses. And we'll all be together, figuring it out. Okay?"

I couldn't think of any pluses to freezing every bit of trash and getting phone calls from dead people. But still, I nodded. And I said, "Okay."

Sunday, November 14

I got in bed with Jo last night. Even though there is not a lot of room in Jo's bed with Jo in it. That's how worried I was.

We slept like this:

It was nice of Jo to let me sleep with her. Even if I got no rest at all. So I didn't **want** to get annoyed with her. But I couldn't help it.

Because right after she woke up, she took her clothes out for the day, including her UNDERWEAR, and put them on my PILLOW. I do not want anyone's underwear on my pillow! So I had to yell at her.

Then, when I opened her top dresser drawer to show her where her underwear actually goes, I saw two tan bras and a bottle of deodorant. Tucked into the side of that drawer.

I closed the drawer and got very quiet.

Bras and deodorant scare me.

At least Jo didn't realize what I saw. Because she had left the room while I was yelling.

When exactly did she get those bras? And the deodorant? Was Mom with her? Was it the most embarrassing day of her entire life?

Why didn't anybody tell me?

What if I decide not to wear deodorant, ever? Will I get all stinky? In my pits?

Later

Mom made a long list of directions for Cousin Carla and put it on the refrigerator, under a magnet. Then she wheeled a gigantic black suitcase out of her room.

"That suitcase is too big," I told her. I stood in the hall, blocking her way to the front door. And hating that gigantic suitcase. Because it meant that Granny's problems were big. <u>And</u> that Mom would be away for too long.

"I always pack too much," Mom said.

That made me feel better. Because it's true. She does always pack too much.

I walked to the door with her, and Jo and Dad joined us, and she gave us all kisses and said she'd call every night. "Right before bed," she said.

"And other times, too?" I said.

"Definitely," she said. "Other times, too."

Then she wheeled her black suitcase out our front door and stepped onto the elevator and was gone.

Later

Dig deep!!

I have to try to dig deep now. Because Dad says it's time for homework. And Friendship Forward is the only homework I have.

I'm not even positive what it means. "Dig deep."

I just asked Dad. He says "dig deep" means "search to the

bottom of your soul." So now I am searching to the bottom of my soul.

I am still searching to the bottom of my soul.

Maybe I've reached the middle of my soul?

I want to watch TV.

Cousin Carla picked us up today. She was waiting
for me in the school lobby after the last bell. I saw
her before she saw me. I stopped at the edge of the
lobby and watched her for a minute.

She was wearing a hoodie with her short skirt
and tights and boots. So at least her cracks were
basically covered.

But still, she was chatting way too much with our
school security guard.

Leave him alone! I thought. He's supposed to be
protecting us!

And then I thought, Please don't say bad words.

And then I thought, I miss Mom.

My heart felt wrung out then. I wanted so badly for

Mom to be there, waiting for me. Wearing her jeans—which do **not** come down too low—and a super-soft sweater. Ready to hug me and ask if I wanted a cookie from the corner store.

I definitely did **not** want Cousin Carla.

I was already in a bad mood, too. Because Nora had sent me this note during English:

Celie—
Lula said that while she was in the bathroom she heard Trina say that your grandma is dying. I'm SO sorry.

Love,
Nora

I *HATED* that note. I wrote Nora right back and said:

My grandma is *NOT DYING*. Trina is an *EVIL LIAR*. Lula knows that! Plus *WHY* is Lula repeating *NASTY, WRONG RUMORS* that she hears in the *BATHROOM?*

Then, right at the end of school, Miss Wilde pulled me and Lula aside to give us a wacko Friendship Forward homework assignment. I still don't understand it. Because the whole time I was glaring at Lula and thinking, Bathroom Rumor Spreader.

I was getting angry with Lula **again** when Cousin Carla finally spotted me. And shouted across the lobby, "Celie! I'm here! Come!"

I didn't know why she couldn't come to me. But I walked over there.

Before she could say anything, I asked her, "Is Granny dying?"

"No!" she cried. Her hand flew to her chest. "Why would you think that?"

"Never mind," I said.

And then Crazy Lunatic Carla did something HORRIBLE!

First, her face got very excited. Then she pointed across the lobby and said to me, "Look!"

I looked—and saw who she was pointing at—and thought, NO! But before I could stop her, Cousin Carla was waving and shouting, "LULA! LULA! OVER HERE!"

I wanted to punch her! And she's a grown-up!

I pulled down on her arm instead and cried, "Stop!"

"What?" Cousin Carla said. Her arm was still up in the air, I was still pulling on it, and Lula was looking over at us. Lots of other people, too.

"Isn't Lula your best friend?" Cousin Carla asked.

"No!" I said. "No she is **not**. Not anymore."

"Oh," Cousin Carla said. She finally put her arm
down.

Then she apologized. At least three times. So I
couldn't get too mad at her.

I couldn't look Lula's way. So I just watched the
school's front door. I wanted to walk out of it. But I
couldn't. Because we had to wait for Jo and stupid
Trina.

They kept not coming, and not coming, and I got
madder and madder.

FINALLY they showed up. They were laughing and
paying no attention to anyone but themselves, and
they knocked right into two kindergartners.

One of those kindergartners fell over.

Jo helped him up, but Trina didn't. She just covered her mouth with her hand and laughed!

"I **hate** Trina," I said, watching her do that.

"REALLY?" Cousin Carla said. She didn't frown or tell me it wasn't nice to hate, like a normal grown-up. Instead, she looked EAGER. Like she wanted me to tell her more.

"Never mind," I said.

And then I had to spend the whole way home trying to stay far away from Mean-a Trina **and** Crazy Cousin Carla.

Later

This is what Jo and Trina did all afternoon in our apartment, instead of studying for their test:

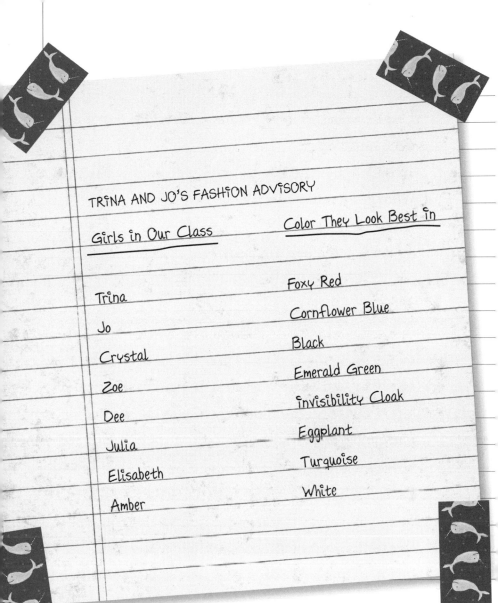

TRINA AND JO'S FASHION ADVISORY

Girls in Our Class	Color They Look Best in
Trina	Foxy Red
Jo	Cornflower Blue
Crystal	Black
Zoe	Emerald Green
Dee	Invisibility Cloak
Julia	Eggplant
Elisabeth	Turquoise
Amber	White

I am not even kidding. I found that list right in the middle of our rug while she and Trina were in the kitchen getting their millionth snack.

I made myself a copy on our printer without them even noticing.

What they said about Dee is so MEAN!

And what the heck is "Foxy Red"?

Later

Foxy Red just made herself a copy of that list and left. **Finally**. Her older brother, Nick, picked her up. He does that sometimes, if it gets dark out. Otherwise, she just goes around by herself. The way Jo wants to.

I hate the way Jo acts around Nick. She talks too fast and laughs too loud and pays **way** too much attention to him.

I guess she has a crush on him. But that's **embarrassing**! Nick is in **high school**! He doesn't care about a sixth grader!

Also, he definitely needs to wash his face.

pimples

Later

Cousin Carla made chicken strips for dinner. Then she ate about a hundred and fifty of them. "I haven't had these in so long!" she said. "They taste **great**!"

It was kind of impressive, how many of those things she ate.

She likes me! She really likes me! Or, at least, strips of me.

Later

I have to do my Friendship Forward homework now.

Here is my crazy assignment:

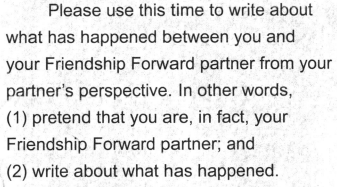

FRIENDSHIP FORWARD

Please use this time to write about what has happened between you and your Friendship Forward partner from your partner's perspective. In other words, (1) pretend that you are, in fact, your Friendship Forward partner; and (2) write about what has happened.

Because I want you to be as forthcoming as possible, you need not turn this in. No one will ever read it. I just ask that you report back to me, on your word of honor, that you have completed it.

Name: Celie

Date: Mon., Nov. 15

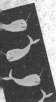

This is a very weird assignment. But I will try to pretend I am Lula.

My name is Lula. I have red hair and brown eyes and I like to wear my sweaters tucked into my pants.

One day a girl named Celie came over to my house. She and I had been best friends forever.

We played in my room for a while. We were writing a skit about narwhals. Then we heard my parents shouting in the living room.

My apartment is not very big. So it was easy to hear the shouts. My mom shouted things like, "You are CONSTANTLY criticizing me! I can NEVER do anything good enough for you! It is a TERRIBLE way to live!" And my dad shouted, "If you just made more of an EFFORT, maybe you would GET THINGS RIGHT!" And then my mom said, "I don't want to live like this. I can't keep living like this!" And my dad said, "No NEED." And then a door slammed. And then the apartment got very quiet. Except we could hear my mom crying.

It was very awkward in my room then. Celie had heard my parents argue before, and she never liked it. But this was definitely the worst ever. She whispered, "Do they get that mad a lot?" I shrugged and said, "I guess."

Then we were quiet for a while. Then Celie whispered, "Do you think they'll get a divorce?" And I said, "NO." Very loudly.

Then I made Celie promise never to say anything about my parents to anyone. Not even her mom or dad or Jo. And she promised.

About a week later I started being incredibly mean to Celie.

The End.

It's me again. Celie.

I'm glad my parents don't fight like that.

Later

I just had the worst conversation of my whole entire life. With Mom. On the phone.

She sounded so tired. And so sad.

She said the doctors did lots of tests on Granny earlier today. They're going to do lots more tomorrow.

"Is she doing well?" I asked Mom. "On the tests?"

Mom waited a second. And then she said, "We don't really know yet."

But I could tell, from her voice. She **did** know. And Granny was **not** doing well.

I told Mom I wanted to talk to Granny then. Because Mom was scaring me. But Mom said, "She's sleeping."

I tried to think of something less scary to talk about.

"Did Granny get my picture?" I asked. "The one of the painting she made me? I sent it last week."

Again Mom paused before answering.

Finally, she said, "Yes, she got it."

Her voice sounded so worried and strange! So I asked, "Is something wrong with it?"

And then Mom said the worst thing. She said: "Granny doesn't remember painting that picture."

Which made no sense at all! How could Granny not remember? She just made that painting a few months ago. And it's a wart medication bottle! That is a very memorable subject!

Mom got another call then. So I had to hold on. When she came back on the line, she said, "It was just Meepsie."

Which made me think of something.

"Did Granny forget where to put her trash?" I said. "Is that why she froze it?"

And then I froze! Because I wasn't supposed to know that Granny froze trash—I only knew from reading Meepsie's email.

Mom didn't even notice.

She just said, "Yes. Granny froze the trash because she forgot what else to do with it."

Questions started flying into my mind. These kinds of questions:

What else would Granny forget? If she forgot what to do with the trash.

What if she forgot what to do with the phone? Or the TV remote?

What if she **microwaved** the TV remote?! It has metal! She could start a fire! She could burn down her whole house!

"Granny can't stay by herself!" I told Mom. "Not if she can't remember what to do with things!"

Mom sighed and said, "Your father and Granny and I are all considering that."

"She **has** to move in with us!" I said. "We can take care of her. **I'll** take care of her."

"Please slow down," Mom said. "We must take this one step at a time. Okay?"

"Okay," I said.

Then Mom made me promise not to tell Jo. "The news needs to come from me or Dad," she said. "Please."

So I promised.

But I shouldn't have. Because I need to talk this through with Jo!

A Little Later

I just looked around our whole apartment. Trying to figure out where Granny should sleep.

The couch in the living room is too lumpy. And the only furniture in Mom's office is her desk and desk chair, plus bookshelves and filing cabinets. So Granny can't sleep there.

I'll give her my bed. And I'll sleep on the air mattress. I think that's the best thing.

deflated

Only, maybe we could get a new air mattress. Because the one we have is leaky.

Later

I just thought of something. What if I invite a friend over and Granny does something strange? Like talk on the phone with a ghost? Or give her toast a bath? What will my friend do?

OR—WAIT! THIS IS SO MUCH WORSE!! What if Jo has **Trina** over and Granny does something? TRINA BETTER NOT MAKE FUN OF MY GRANNY. **EVER.** Or I will get her whole entire skinny jeans collection and cut it into shreds. I really will.

I need to talk to Dad. Especially since I can't talk to Jo. But Cousin Carla says he has a meeting and won't be home until very late. That's when she'll go to her home, to sleep.

Why can't grown-ups meet during the day? Why do they **ever** have to meet after dark?

Waiting for Dad

So very late

Dad's **still** not home. I have Granny's tablecloth in bed with me. I'm going to sleep with it spread right over me. Even though Mom hasn't had a chance to wash it yet.

I think the egg yolk stain might be starting to stink.

I don't care. I'll just put that part down by my feet.

Tuesday, November 16

I finally got to talk to Dad this morning. After we'd eaten breakfast and Jo had gotten in the shower. But that conversation did not go well!

Dad sat in my room with me. I told him the whole story of my phone call with Mom. I told him how Mom had said that Granny's test results were going to be bad, and that Granny had forgotten what to do with trash, and that Granny might move in with us.

Then I asked him, "What else is Granny going to forget? I don't understand. And can she **please** move in with us?"

I'd thought Dad would explain everything, very patiently. And probably make me laugh a little.

Instead, he didn't say anything at all for a second.

And I could tell from his face—something had made him mad.

"What?" I asked him. "Why are you looking that way? What did I do?"

He shook his head and smiled a little. It was not a convincing smile.

"You did not do anything," he said. "And I promise we will figure everything out. As soon as we have Granny's test results."

Then he stood up and started walking toward my door. Which made me mad. Because he hadn't explained anything at all!

And then he startled me! Just as I was about to tell him how frustrating he was being, he reached out and **punched** my punching bag. Very hard. And then he walked out of my room.

I think I have to get
Dad a journal. So
he can work
out his feelings
that way.
Because I
do **not** like
seeing him
punch when
he is mad.

A tiny Bit Later

Dad just took the phone into his room and shut
the door. I knew he was going to call Mom. To talk
about what I'd just told him.

So I sat in the hallway, right outside that door, and
tried to listen in. Even though both of us should've
been getting dressed. Because we were running out
of time before school.

I could only hear parts of sentences. But those parts were bad enough.

I heard:
"... *realize* you're worried and exhausted, but ..."

and
"... *not right* to burden Celie until ..."

and
"... make decisions together *first* before telling her ..."

and
"... You're mischaracterizing what I said!"

His voice got LOUD at the end. But I couldn't stay and write more down. Because I heard his footsteps, heading right toward me. So I rushed away from there. Now I have to hurry and get dressed. Bye.

Later, After school

I had such bad thoughts this morning. I was supposed to be learning how to tell time in Spanish. But I couldn't focus on that, not even for a second. Because I kept thinking about Mom and Dad.

These were the thoughts that kept spinning through my head: Dad is so mad at Mom now. And she must be mad at him, too. They were definitely yelling at each other at the end of that call. I **hate** that they're fighting. I hate that it's my fault. I should never have told Dad what Mom said to me. Why couldn't I just be quiet? How long will they stay mad?

Eventually, during all that thinking, I ended up looking at Lula. Because she sits right in front of me in Spanish.

I thought then: I wonder if Lula feels this yucky a lot, worrying about her parents yelling at each other. And I wonder if she ever feels like their fighting is her fault.

Then I made a decision.

I got a piece of paper and a pen out of my desk, and I wrote Lula a note. Then I folded it really tight and leaned far forward and dropped it quickly on her desk.

After I sat back up again, I got very nervous! Because I hadn't written to Lula or talked to her in so long. What if she didn't write back?

But she **did** write back. Which was good. Only, what she said made me upset!

We went back and forth.

Lula —

I'm sorry that your parents fight. And also, I
hope they aren't fighting anymore.

Celie

Celie—

Why did you tell Nora about the fighting?
You promised you wouldn't!

From,
Lula

I **NEVER** told Nora! **EVER!** Why would you
think that?

You passed that note to her, that morning. You looked right at me when you were writing it. And Nora looked like she was going to cry when she read it. And after she read it, she was very, very nice to me. Just like she knew.

WHAT MORNING?! I DON'T KNOW WHAT YOU'RE TALKING ABOUT! AND I DON'T KNOW WHY NORA WAS BEING VERY NICE! She's a nice person! I write notes to her all the time, but I never wrote to her about your parents! NEVER EVER! You can ask Nora!

Oh.
Sorry.
But you did stop wanting to come to my house. After that fight you saw. Every single time I asked you over after that, you said, "Can we go to my house instead?" So I knew you didn't like being at my house, with my parents, anymore.

I had to stop writing after that last note. Because she was right. I __had__ stopped wanting to go to her house.

That must have made her feel so bad. That's how __I'd__ feel, if she stopped coming to my house because of my parents. Or because of Granny.

I didn't write her back. Instead I turned and waited until she looked over at me. Then, as clearly as I could, I mouthed the words, "I'm very sorry."

She nodded.

And that was the end of our talking for the whole day. Because after that Lula never passed me another note or came up and said something to me. She just talked to Violet and walked from class to class with Violet and went to the bathroom with Violet. As usual.

I thought about passing Lula another note. But I couldn't think of anything else to say.

A Little Later

Cousin Carla just did a **ridiculous** thing! She pointed at the boots Jo's wearing and said, "I **love** those! Want to let me borrow them? They look about my size. And they're **adorable**!"

That woman is FORTY! Why does she want to wear a SIXTH GRADER'S shoes??

Jo didn't know <u>what</u> to do. She looked from her boots to Cousin Carla and said, "Uh . . ."

I came to the rescue! I said, "Mom doesn't let us share shoes. Because of foot fungus. Which is very contagious."

Cousin Carla made a funny face, like she didn't enjoy thinking about foot fungus. "Maybe I'll just buy some," she said.

"Good idea," I said.

Jo told me later that she doesn't want Cousin Carla showing up in our school lobby wearing matching boots. And probably telling the whole world, "Look! Don't we both have great taste!"

That <u>would</u> be embarrassing. But at least Jo's boots are safe.

Cousin Carla

STILL TUESDAY
(AFTER ANOTHER CHICKEN
STRIPS DINNER)

I was just punching my punching bag, trying to figure out what to do about Lula. I kept hoping and hoping she'd call me and say, "Want to come over sometime?" So I could say, "Yes! I definitely do! We can **always** hang out over there, if you want."

And then our phone rang! So I yanked off my gloves and ran to Mom's office and picked up the phone. All for nothing. Because it was just stupid Trina, calling for Jo.

Jo came and took the phone. I wanted to stop punching and thinking about Lula. So I sat in the hall instead and listened to Jo talking.

I did not like what I heard!

Jo said:

"Sure, I remember that list—we just made it a couple of days ago. Why?"

and

"I don't know. No, actually, I don't think so. That doesn't seem right."

and

"Because of the invisibility cloak thing. That seems so mean, and I don't want to be mean."

and

"Let's talk about it when we see each other, in person. We can talk about it tomorrow."

and

"No, you can't just do it without me. My name's on there, too."

and

"Fine. Bye."

It sounded like Jo threw the phone on the desk then.

I tried to hurry out of the hall, so Jo wouldn't know I'd listened. But I didn't have time to do anything except start crawling. I must've looked very guilty. But it didn't matter. Jo paid no attention to me. She just rushed to our room and slammed the door.

Very close to bedtime now

I'm still thinking about that call.

Trina must've been talking about their stupid Fashion Advisory. But what mean thing does she want to do with it? Can Jo stop her? Is Jo going to give in?

I **told** her not to be friends with Foxy Red.

I don't like this.

I still wish it had been Lula who'd called, instead of evil Trina.

Black is the color of my mood.

Wednesday, November 17

Mrs. McElhaney asked us to pick partners in Literature Circle this morning. I thought about asking Lula. I got a little nervous, thinking, I could ask her. I'll just ask her.

But she was sitting next to Violet. And the second Mrs. McElhaney told us to choose someone, Violet picked Lula.

So I wasn't partners with Lula.

She was nice to me in Science, though. When she passed my desk on her way to the bathroom. She looked right at me and smiled. I liked that a lot.

And then, when Lula came back, she stopped at my desk and whispered something! She whispered, "Something weird's happening with Jo and Trina by the sixth-grade lockers."

So I told Mrs. McElhaney I had to go to the bathroom. And I ran to the sixth-grade lockers.

Jo and Trina were still there. Jo was holding a sheet of paper high above her head and trying to keep it from Trina, who was on her tiptoes, grabbing at it.

Then Trina stepped back for a second.

"Why do you even **care**?" she said to Jo in a very nasty voice. "Is Dee your new best friend?"

"No, but that doesn't mean it's okay to put this list on her locker!" Jo said.

"You shouldn't have helped me make it, then," Trina said.

"I wish I hadn't," Jo said. She started ripping that list up.

I was so proud of Jo for doing that! But then

Trina said, "I can always write it up again, you big lame-o."

She paused for a second. Then she said, "Speaking of lame, Nick totally knows you have a crush on him. He thinks it's **pathetic.**"

Then she turned and walked away.

I ran to Jo.

"You're not one bit pathetic," I told her. "You just stood up to a terrible person."

Jo smiled a little.

"Thanks," she said. "But she'll probably just make the list again. I wish I could stand here and guard Dee's locker forever and ever, but I can't."

"At least you stopped Trina for now," I said.

She shook her head.

I hated seeing her sad because of nasty evil Trina.

"You're a hero, not a lame-o," I told her. She laughed a little. Then we both had to go back to class.

I couldn't think about science at all, though. I could only think, How are we going to keep Trina from posting the list again?

But then I forgot about that for a while. Because Lula and I started passing notes! I collected them all. I had to sneak the ones that I'd passed to Lula out of the trashcan after everyone else had left the room. (I saw her drop them in there, super-slyly, on her way out.) It was yucky and scary, picking through that trash, looking all around me, worrying that someone would come back in. But I did it.

Here's our whole conversation:

C—

Is everything okay with Jo?

Lula

Sort of.
Thanks for telling me they were
out there.

Sure. I wanted to tell you something
else, too. You don't have to come to
my house anymore. I know my parents
mess everything up.

No! I <u>**want**</u> to come to your house! We can ignore your parents! I ignore mine all the time.

No, you don't! Your parents are so great.

Yes, I do! I did it just the other night, at dinner. My dad said to stop talking about cracks in boobs and butts, and I ignored him.

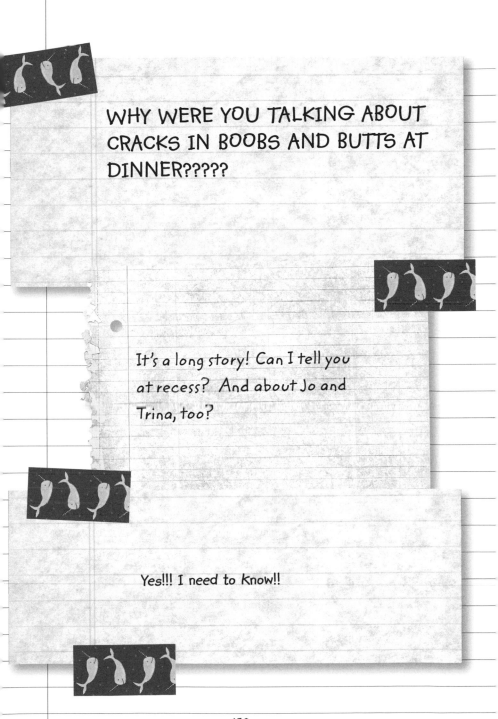

WHY WERE YOU TALKING ABOUT CRACKS IN BOOBS AND BUTTS AT DINNER?????

It's a long story! Can I tell you at recess? And about Jo and Trina, too?

Yes!!! I need to know!!

Just the idea of talking to Lula at recess again. Just that idea, by itself. It made me so happy.

Later

I just had a nice conversation with Mom on the phone. I miss her. I want her to come home. I listened very carefully to her voice at first. To see if she sounded upset because she'd been fighting with Dad. Or mad at me because I caused the fighting with Dad. But she just sounded happy to talk to me.

I told her about recess and how Lula and I sat on the swings together and talked.

"So the two of you have worked it out!" she said, sounding so relieved.

"I hope so," I said.

I told her about keeping Cousin Carla from wearing Jo's boots, too. But I didn't tell her about the epic battle between Jo and Trina. Because Jo might get in trouble if Mom and Dad find out that she helped make that invisibility cloak list in the first place.

Plus, I have an idea for making sure Trina doesn't post the list again. But I know Mom would **hate** my idea. So I decided to stay away from that whole topic.

Thursday, November 18

Dad asked me and Jo to come sit with him in the living room this morning, before breakfast. "I have some news," he said.

Of course I knew it had to be about Granny. So I said, very quickly, "Good news or bad news?"

I expected him to say, "Bad news." Because his face looked serious.

Instead, he said, "Complicated news."

Then he explained that the Louisiana doctors still weren't positive what was wrong with Granny. "I'd hoped there might be an easy solution," he said. "Like a vitamin deficiency in her diet." He smiled a little. "I'd hoped she just needed to eat more bananas."

I had no idea what he was talking about. Why

would **bananas** help? But before I could ask, he kept going.

"Unfortunately there's no easy solution **or** easy diagnosis," he said. "It's going to take a long time to figure out exactly what's wrong with Granny and how we can best help her. That's the bad part of the news."

"What's the good part?" Jo asked.

"The good part is that Granny is going to come stay with us now," Dad said. "At least for a while. There are many excellent doctors here, and this way we can be with her and watch over her."

"She can sleep in my bed!" I said. "I'll use an air mattress. Only, Jo has to stop leaving her underwear and dirty socks on that bed. Once it's Granny's."

"I would never do that to Granny!" Jo said.

"You do it to **me**!" I said. "Why is okay to do it to **me**?"

"Girls!" Dad said. "There's absolutely no need to fight. We're going to convert Mom's office into a bedroom for Granny. I do not believe Jo has ever left her underwear strewn around Mom's office. But, just so we're perfectly clear—Jo, will you solemnly swear that you will never strew your underwear around Granny's new bedroom?"

"Yes," Jo said. "I solemnly swear."

"What about on my pillow?" I said. "Are you still going to strew your underwear there?"

"You make everything about **you**," Jo said.

"The natives are getting restless!" Dad said. "This meeting is adjourned."

Then he stood up and walked over to me and kissed my cheek and said, "Thank you for offering your bed."

Then he kissed Jo's cheek and said, "Thank you for your underwear oath."

Then he stepped back a little and looked at the two of us.

And he said, "I'm so proud of you both."

Later

Lots happened this afternoon! First, in the lobby
after school ended, Lula asked if I could come over.
Which made me very happy, but only for a second.
Because Crazy EMBARRASSING Cousin Carla
heard, and clapped her hands together, and said,
"Are you two best friends again? How **nice**!"

I couldn't even look at Lula then! Because I still
don't know what kind of friends we are. It's too soon
to know that. We just started talking again! WHY
DID COUSIN CARLA HAVE TO ASK?

I glared at Crazy Cousin Carla. Then I said, "Would
you please just tell me if I can go?"

"Of course you can go!" she said.

So I went home with Lula and her mom. Her dad
wasn't there, which was a very big relief. Because

I'm not sure how I should act if her parents start fighting. I just know not to write a note to **anyone** about **anything** the next day.

I liked seeing Lula's room again. I had missed it, without even realizing. I like the tall windows. And I like sitting with Lula on the floor between her twin beds, cross-legged. The carpet is so soft.

I told her my idea for making sure Trina doesn't post the list again. She loved it, and she helped me plan it. Here is a copy of what we're going to slip into Trina's locker:

TRINA!
RIP UP YOUR STUPID LIST!
IF YOU DO NOT, WE WILL POST
THIS PICTURE ALL OVER THE PLACE.

This is Trina. She thinks she is foxy. She is in love with skinny jeans. She wants to marry them.

I just did a weird thing while Jo
was taking a shower.

I tried on her deodorant.

Deodorant is
cold and wet!
And a little
sticky. I had to
hold my arms
out from my
sides and flap
them up and
down. To get that
stuff to dry.

I do not understand how
people wear
it every day. I
definitely do not.

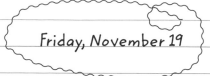

Friday, November 19

We did it! Lula and I slid our Trina-wants-to-marry-skinny-jeans note into her locker this morning. I don't think anyone saw us. But Trina will probably know it's from me. I hope she's scared.

I hope we don't get in trouble.

I just had a worrying thought. What if we end up in Friendship Forward with **Trina**? Yuck. I **never, ever** want to dig deep about Trina.

We're about to go shopping. Dad and Jo and me.
We're just waiting for Jo to finish talking on the
phone to a girl in her class named Amber. She's
always seemed nice.

They've been on that call forever. But I am waiting
very patiently. Because Jo needs a nice new friend.

When we finally leave, we're going to pick out pretty
sheets and a comforter for Granny. I think they
should be blue and white. To match her tablecloth.
Which I'm planning to get nice and clean and then
put right over Mom's desk.

We're still not sure exactly what day Granny's
moving in. But I'm going to ask Delores to make her
famous brownies for her, whenever that day is.

I know Lula will ignore Granny's forgetting, the

way I'm planning to ignore her parents' fighting.

None of us cares one bit if Granny freezes pink sponge curlers or talks to the dead. We're going to make her a home.

Here's a look at Celie's next adventure,

Secrets Out

JOURNAL

PUT THIS JOURNAL
DOWN RIGHT NOW.
DO NOT TURN
THE PAGE.
IT IS **<u>PRIVATE</u>**.

That especially means you,
Josephine Rosalie Altman. If
you do not put this right back
where you found it and walk
away, I will tell your whole grade
that when you eat strawberries
you get a rash on your tushy.

I am not kidding, Jo.
No, I definitely am not.

In this new book, Celie discovers that keeping secrets is hard . . . really hard.

And even though she tries her best, she runs into some sticky situations. Like:

★ That time she ends up with her best friend Lula's private notes, even though she probably should have left them where she found them (unread and in the trash)

★ Or when she reads her sister Jo's texts (and finds out Jo is going on a date! A real live date)

★ Or, worst of all, when something really bad happens and she has to lie to her mom and dad (but only to protect someone she loves!)

What do you do when it feels like everything around you is just getting more and more complicated? And who do you turn to when you're keeping so many secrets from everyone?

It's a good thing Granny bought Celie a new diary. Because it feels like this is the only safe place for her to try to figure everything out.